YOUR FAVOURITE FLINTSTONES STORY COLLECTION

DEAN

CONTENTS

Caught in the Act

On Sunday nights the Flintstones and Rubbles always watched their favourite programme on television.

"The show that catches people unaware - *Peek-a-Boo Camera*," said the TV announcer. "Here's your host, Pete Moss!"

"There's nothing like watching people act silly," Fred chuckled.

"Speaking of acting silly, we are still going dancing next Saturday, aren't we?" asked Wilma.

"Of course," Betty replied. "Barney and I have been looking forward to it."

"Good. I want it to be a really special evening," said Wilma. "It's been ages since we've all been dancing."

The telephone rang just then. "Flintstone, this is the Grand Buffalo," said a deep voice on the telephone.

"The G-Grand Buffalo?" Fred reached into the cupboard for his Water Buffalo hat.

WHATEVER YOU SAY, GRAND BUFFALO, SIR.

"There's a special Water Buffalo party next Saturday. Tell Rubble, will you?" ordered the Grand Buffalo, and rang off.

Fred rejoined the others in the lounge. "Wilma, er, I'm afraid there's a special Water Buffalo...um..." Fred paused, at a loss for words, "...meeting. Yeah, that's it. There's a special Water Buffalo club meeting next Saturday night."

Wilma sighed. "Well, I guess we can go dancing another time."

Fred and Barney had a great time at the party on Saturday night.

They didn't know it, but behind the scenes Pete Moss was filming them for *Peek-a-Boo Camera.*

"Those two are so funny," Pete Moss laughed. "This will be my best show yet." He went on stage to introduce himself. "Hi there, TV fans. Recognise me?"

"Why you're - you're..." Fred stammered.

"That's right! I'm Pete Moss and you're on *Peek-a-Boo Camera*!"

"Are we really going to be on *Peek-a-Boo Camera?*" asked Barney.

"You certainly are," replied Pete. "You'll be on tomorrow's show. But first you must sign these forms to make it all legal."

"No problem," said Fred as he and Barney signed the forms.

"Great party, wasn't it?" said Barney when they arrived home. "I can't wait until Betty and Wilma see us on *Peek-a-Boo Camera.*"

Fred grinned, then suddenly his grin turned into a frown. "Barney, we can't let Wilma and Betty see us on TV! They think we were at a Water Buffalo meeting, not a party!"

Pete was snoring gently. Fred tapped on the window and Pete woke with a start.

GEE, IT'S A LONG WAY DOWN.

"Flintstone, what do you want?"

"Barney and I want to be off the show," said Fred.

"Sorry," said Pete. "You signed the forms. You've got no choice now. See you on *Peek-a-Boo Camera,* Flintstone."

FRED, WHAT ARE WE GOING TO DO?

WE'LL HAVE TO EXPLAIN TO PETE MOSS.

MR MOSS, I'VE GOT TO TALK TO YOU.

They dashed over to the hotel where Pete Moss was staying, but the doorman wouldn't let them in. Luckily, Fred spotted a fire escape ladder leading right up to Pete's window on the top floor.

Down on the ground, Barney saw a hotel security guard coming towards them.

"Hold on tight, Fred!" he shouted, and raced away, still clutching the ladder in his hands with Fred clinging on tightly.

"Look out!" yelled Fred.

It was too late. The ladder crashed and folded in half, leaving Fred dangling upside down from the rungs.

The next day Fred asked Wilma if she wanted to go out dancing.

"It will make up for missing last night," said Fred. "We'll ask Barney and Betty to come with us, and we'll dance all night.

How about it, Wilma?"

"You're sweet, Fred," Wilma replied. "But I've already invited Betty and Barney over to watch *Peek-a-Boo Camera*."

Fred sighed miserably. He'd better come up with a plan - and quickly - or he'd be in big trouble!

At last Fred came up with a plan. He and Barney disguised themselves as TV repairmen. Fred knocked on the door.

"Hello," he said. "We're from Bedrock Televisions. Your husband asked me to come round to take your TV for a service."

"Uh-oh," said Barney. He went to replace the TV set, but his feet got tangled in the cord and the TV crashed to the floor!

Wilma phoned Betty. "Fred and Barney have just broken our television. Is it okay if we watch *Peek-a-Boo Camera* at your house?"

"That Fred. He never tells me anything," said Wilma. "Come in then."

Barney picked up the TV. As he and Fred turned to leave, Dino suddenly rushed over to greet Fred, pulling off his disguise.

"Fred?!" exclaimed Wilma in surprise.

"Heh, heh. Hi, Wilma," said Fred.

10

"Sure," said Betty. But as she spoke, Barney reached through the window behind her and grabbed the TV. "Wilma, someone has stolen our TV set!" Betty cried.

Fred and Barney hopped into the car with the TV, not realising that they'd forgotten to unplug it. The car zoomed off, stretching the flex taut until finally the TV went hurtling backwards, shattering into little pieces!

"I don't understand you boys," said Wilma that evening. "What have you got against television all of a sudden?"

"Yes, now we've missed *Peek-a-Boo Camera*," Betty added.

Fred grinned. "Gee, that's a shame."

A week later, the Flintstones and Rubbles gathered round as usual to watch *Peek-a-Boo Camera*. "I like your new television set," Betty remarked.

"Oh thanks," Wilma replied. "Look, here comes Pete Moss."

"Well, we've certainly had a big response to last week's show," Pete paused dramatically. "So, we're going to repeat it for you. Here they are - the waltzing Water Buffalos!"

Fred and Barney looked at each other in horror as they saw themselves dancing across the TV screen.

Wilma glared at Fred. Fred edged towards the door, then raced outside with Wilma in hot pursuit.

"You come back here, Fred, or I'll ring Pete Moss," called Wilma. "This will make a great episode for *Peek-a-Boo Camera!*"

Dino's Double

"Well, that's another day's work over," said Fred as he and Barney drove home. "I can't wait to get home to relax with Wilma and Pebbles."

Fred slowed down to cross the bridge. "Oh no," he said suddenly, glancing at the string tied round his finger. "I knew I'd forgotten something."

"Something for Pebbles, maybe?" Barney suggested.

"Yeah, that's it! Something for Pebbles," said Fred, smiling at the thought of his baby daughter.

At home, Wilma gave Dino a special bone. "Happy anniversary, Dino," she said. Pebbles clapped and Dino barked happily.

"You're such a big help in taking care of Pebbles," Wilma added. "You're just like one of the family, Dino."

Dino rushed to greet Fred at the door. "Down boy," ordered Fred. He gave Pebbles her gift. "Look what Daddy has for you, Pebbles."

He rushed to set up the camera as Pebbles cuddled her new doll.

"Didn't you get any dinosaur toys, Fred?" Wilma asked.

"Why would I get dinosaur toys for Pebbles?" Fred replied.

"Fred, how could you forget Dino's first anniversary with us?" Wilma asked later.

Fred snapped his fingers. "*That's* what the string was for."

"Yes, Fred, and you forgot anyway," said Wilma. "Why don't you apologise to Dino?"

Dino was watching over Pebbles while she rocked happily in her cradle. Suddenly, Pebbles rocked a little too hard. The cradle tipped dangerously, and was about to topple over with Pebbles inside it when Dino leaped to the rescue and caught her in his mouth!

Fred entered just in time to see Dino grab Pebbles. "Dino, put Pebbles down!" he yelled. "This is the last straw. From now on, you sleep outside."

The next morning, Wilma went out to give Dino his breakfast. But Dino wasn't there.

Reluctantly, Fred searched the garden for Dino. "He's definitely gone," Fred declared. "Looks like he's run away."

POOR DINO, OUT THERE ALL ALONE.

Pebbles burst into tears.

"I'm sorry Dino, wherever you are," said Fred, a tear trickling down his cheek.

Meanwhile, Dino was wandering around town looking for a new home.

Oh Pebbles, he thought sadly, *how I miss you.*

Pebbles refused to eat anything until Dino came home.

"We've looked everywhere," said Fred, arriving home with Barney. They'd driven around town searching for Dino.

"No luck, I'm afraid," said Barney, "but we did put an advert in the newspaper."

Wilma sighed. "We've just got to find Dino. I don't know what we'll do without him."

15

Just then the doorbell rang. Three people stood at the door, all with dinosaurs looking exactly like Dino.

"Here's your pet," they all said as they entered. "Where's my reward?"

Fred looked at the three dinosaurs. Which was the real Dino?

But Pebbles had already solved the problem. She crawled past the three dinosaurs and burst into tears again.

So once more Fred and Barney went in search of Dino.

"Barney, look in that garden!" exclaimed Fred. "It's Dino. He's been kidnapped."

"Lots of dinosaurs around here are purple with spots," Barney pointed out.

The dinosaur growled at Fred.

"See Barney?" said Fred. "Dino's mad at me because I yelled at him."

Just then a man ran out of the house. "Hey, you leave Rocky alone or I'll ring the police!" he shouted.

"That's my Dino," Fred declared. "And I want him back."

"I'm sorry gentlemen, but you must be mistaken," the man said. He turned to the dinosaur. "Rocky, show these two men the way out."

At home, Fred made a plan.
"We've got to get Dino back, Barney. And I know how," he said.

"But Fred, I don't think that dinosaur was Dino," said Barney.

"Course it was," Fred insisted. "I'll sleep in Dino's shed for a week if that wasn't Dino. Now listen Barney, this is what we're going to do..."

If only Fred had known that the real Dino was still wandering the streets, hungry and lonely.

Fred and Barney went back to the house where they'd seen the dinosaur.

"When I say 'now', you slip the sack over Dino's head and I'll grab him," Fred told Barney.

The plan worked perfectly until the dinosaur started howling.

"Be quiet, Dino," Fred whispered. "We've come to rescue you."

The dinosaur howled even louder, waking up his owner.

"Put my dinosaur down, you thieves!" the man cried. "Police! Help, police!"

Fred and Barney sped off in the car, with the dinosaur wriggling on Barney's lap.

"We did it!" Fred exclaimed.

But from a distance, Barney heard a siren rapidly gaining on them.

"Uh, Fred, sounds like the police behind us," he said.

"So what? All I did was take back my own pet dinosaur," Fred replied.

"I hope you're right," said Barney.

"I told you, if this dinosaur isn't Dino, I'll sleep in Dino's shed. That's how sure I am," Fred declared, as the police officer approached the car.

Wilma, Betty and Pebbles went down to the police station to bail out Fred. He was still trying to convince the angry owner that the dinosaur was really Dino. "His name is Rocky and he's my dinosaur," the man retorted.

"Do you see that sweet little girl?" Fred asked. "She hasn't eaten a thing since you took Dino."

Pebbles looked at Rocky and burst into tears. That wasn't her dinosaur!

Then, a miracle happened. Dino was wandering by the police station looking for a few morsels of food. He looked in the window and saw his precious Pebbles. He raced into the station.

Everyone was glad to have Dino home again, even Fred.

"Gee Fred, when you make a bet, you really go through with it," said Barney.

"A bargain is a bargain," said Fred.

"Besides, I've got to admit it - our Dino is one in a million."

Mistaken Identities

The Flintstones and the Rubbles were having a pleasant evening together.

"Did you know that the Honeyrock Hotel has been redecorated?" Wilma remarked. "It looks lovely."

"What memories," said Barney. "The Honeyrock Hotel is where Betty and I first met."

"Wilma and I met there too," Fred reminded him. "Sixteen years ago."

Wilma sighed. "I'll never forget that wonderful summer."

"Neither will I," said Fred. . .

The hotel manager snapped his fingers. "Bellhop, take this luggage to Room 402."

"Yes sir," said Fred. He turned to Barney. "Assistant bellhop, take this luggage to Room 402."

"Uh, okay, Fred," replied Barney, gathering up the cases.

Fred followed with the hand luggage.

In the hotel dining room, Wilma and Betty started their first day as waitresses.

"Remember," said the manager, "into the kitchen through IN and out through OUT."

Everything went smoothly - until Betty came out of the kitchen through IN.

CRASH!

Fred and Barney had the afternoon off.

"You ready, Fred?" asked Barney.

"Almost," Fred replied. "I want to look my best in case we meet some beautiful, rich girls. After all, the Honeyrock Hotel is the playground of the wealthy."

HOW DO I LOOK, BARNEY?

As it happened, Wilma and Betty had the afternoon off too.

"Let's go, Betty," Wilma said.

"I want to look my best, Wilma," Betty replied. "Suppose I meet a rich, handsome young man?"

"Then I hope you'll ask him if he has a friend for me," Wilma giggled.

As Fred and Barney wandered out of the hotel, a man stopped them.

"Would you be good enough to park my car for me?" the man asked. "I'm late for a meeting of the Millionaire's Club."

THIS IS SOME CAR!

IT'S A TOP OF THE LINE JAGUSAURUS.

"Yes sir!" said Fred and Barney together, gazing at the car with envy.

Wilma and Betty walked past the hotel swimming pool and out to the car park.

"Look at that gorgeous car," Wilma remarked. She hopped inside.

Betty climbed in after her friend. "Wilma, what are we doing here?"

"Practising to be millionaires," Wilma replied. "Isn't it fun?"

"Hey Fred, look at those beautiful girls," Barney exclaimed.

"I'm looking, I'm looking!" Fred replied. He parked the car right next to Wilma and Betty. "Hi there, girls."

We're in trouble now, Betty thought. But Wilma was already smiling at Fred.

"Hello. That's a lovely car you've got."

"Oh it's not —" Fred began. "It's not as nice as yours. Are you girls staying at the hotel?"

"Of course, Fred," Barney answered. "Where else would millionaires stay?"

Wilma and Betty looked at each other.

"Oh, how quaint," said Betty.

The movie was about two millionaires in love. But then the hero admitted that he wasn't a millionaire at all.

Fred and Barney frowned.

Then the heroine confessed that she wasn't a millionaire either.

Wilma and Betty wanted to disappear.

The two couples spent as much time together as possible. They rode the bus into town so often the bus driver got to know them by name. They went dancing and dining, saw a few more movies and even played mini golf.

When they had all introduced themselves, Fred suggested going to the cinema.

"What fun!" Wilma agreed. "Shall we take your car? Mine is too small to fit all of us." She laughed nervously.

Fred hesitated. "I've got an idea. Why don't we take a bus? It'll be an adventure, don't you think?"

Wilma wrote to her mother about Fred.

A few days later, Fred was on duty.

He went to help one of the guests with her luggage, but she wouldn't let go of her suitcase.

"That's okay, sonny. I'll take it myself," the woman insisted.

"It's no bother," Fred replied. "I'm here to be of service."

As they struggled over the suitcase, the catch snapped open!

MY FUTURE SON-IN-LAW IS GOING TO HEAR ABOUT THIS. HE'S A MILLIONAIRE, YOU KNOW.

IF THOSE BOYS REALLY LOVE YOU, THEY'LL UNDERSTAND.

YOU'RE RIGHT. WE'LL TELL THEM THE TRUTH.

Wilma and Betty were relaxing before work.

"I wish the boys would invite us to that fancy dress party tonight," Wilma said.

"Stop wishing. We'll be working at the party, remember?" Betty replied.

There was a knock on the door.

"Mother!" Wilma exclaimed.

"Hello dear," her mother said. "I've come to see if your millionaire boyfriend is as wonderful as you say."

Wilma sighed. "Oh, he is wonderful. But when he finds out I've been deceiving him, he'll probably board his yacht and sail out of my life forever."

With the guests at the fancy dress party, it was a quiet night for Fred and Barney.

"When are we going to tell those nice girls the truth, Fred?" Barney asked.

"I don't know," Fred said glumly. "If we tell them that we're bellhops and not millionaires, it will be 'Goodbye, Fred'."

"And 'Goodbye, Barney'," Barney added.

"Hey, let's take a peek at the fancy dress party," Fred suggested. "Maybe that will cheer us up."

DO YOU SEE WHAT I SEE, FRED ?

WILMA, LOOK WHO JUST WALKED IN.

At the fancy dress party, Fred and Barney spotted Wilma and Betty - dressed as waitresses!

"Hi, girls!" said Fred. "Nice costumes. Waitresses - that's really original."

"S-so are yours," Wilma replied. "I'd never have thought of you as a bellhop."

"Shall we dance?" Fred suggested.

Wilma hesitated. She was supposed to be working, but one dance couldn't hurt. It would give her a chance to confess.

"Fred," said Wilma, "we've got to talk."

"Me first, Wilma," Fred said. "You see -"

But just then they were interrupted by the hotel manager.

"M-Mr Stonyface, er, lovely party," said Fred. "I always like fancy dress."

Mr Stonyface didn't even crack a smile. "You're fired!" he shouted.

"I'll never see Fred again," sobbed Wilma as they left the hotel.

"Good riddance to that awful phoney millionaire," her mother replied.

"I was just as dishonest as he was," Wilma declared. "Besides, I love him."

"And I love Barney," Betty added sadly.

Just then they noticed two familiar figures.

"Mother, stop!" shouted Wilma. "Where are you going, boys?" she asked.

Fred grinned. "Wherever you're going, Wilma, that's where I want to be."

He hopped in the car, and they drove off to Bedrock and lived happily ever after. . .

"That was a wonderful summer, wasn't it?" Wilma remarked.

"A summer to remember," Betty agreed.

"Well, I'll never forget it," said Fred. "And you know what, Wilma? I wouldn't swap you for a million dollars!"

Time Travellers

Pebbles and Bamm-Bamm liked the roller coaster best.

"Look - free babysitting," Barney said, pointing to a sign.

"How about it, kids?" asked Fred.

Pebbles and Bamm-Bamm nodded excitedly. The octopus babysitter looked like fun!

"I don't think we need to worry about Pebbles and Bamm-Bamm," Wilma laughed. "Let's go and see the rest of the fair."

The Flintstones and the Rubbles were spending the day at the Bedrock Fair. They played games at the arcade, visited Kiddyland and went on some wild rides!

"Has anyone tried the machine yet?" asked Wilma.

"Not yet," the inventor replied. "You'll be the first. Isn't that exciting?"

Barney was doubtful. "Travelling to the future sounds scary to me."

"We can't travel to the future. It hasn't happened yet," declared Fred.

Fred, Wilma, Barney and Betty all squeezed into the time machine.

"I'll shut my eyes and spin the dial," said the inventor to himself.

He looked through the peephole.

"Those people are gone! My time machine really works!" he shouted with glee.

They headed for the House of Tomorrow. Inside, they found a man working on a strange-looking contraption.

"Would you like a trip to the future?" he asked. "Step into my time machine."

Fred chuckled. "Sounds like fun."

COME ON. IT'S JUST A TRICK.

Suddenly, the Flintstones and Rubbles were spinning through space.

"Don't worry everybody," said Fred calmly. "This is all fake."

Then they landed with a bump.

"Where are we?" asked Wilma.

"That sign says we're in Rome," said Barney. "Look at that stadium over there."

"Barney, that's not a real stadium. It's just a picture," Fred insisted.

"Let's take a look anyway," said Barney.

Wilma and Betty walked through the entrance of the stadium, but Fred and Barney were stopped by the guard.

"The gladiators' entrance is that way," said the guard, pointing them in the other direction.

"J-just what we were looking for, wasn't it Fred?" Barney stammered.

"Where are the boys?" Betty asked.

"I don't know. Maybe they went to get popcorn." Suddenly, Wilma gasped. "Betty, look down there! It's Fred and Barney!"

Down in the arena, Fred was telling Barney about the inventor's trick time machine when two lionasaurs came charging towards them.

"Fred, look out!" warned Barney.

"Nonsense, Barney," Fred said calmly. "They're not real."

29

One of the lionasaurs glared at Fred, then with one swipe of his paw, tore the seat off Fred's tunic.

"B-Barney, these lionasaurs are real!" Fred yelped in surprise.

"I told you, Fred," said Barney. "That time machine was no trick."

Back at the House of Tomorrow, the inventor had a sudden thought.

"I'd better bring those people back to the present now..."

This time they landed on a boat.

"I am Captain Christopher Columbus," a man told them. "Where are your tickets?"

"We paid to get into the fair," said Wilma. "We thought all the rides were included."

Columbus shook his head in dismay. "Stowaways, eh? You'll have to work for your passage then."

The Flintstones and Rubbles soon found themselves scrubbing the deck.

"I thought this fair was supposed to be fun," Barney complained. "Where are we going anyway?"

"We are going around the world," Columbus told him. "My crew thinks we're going to fall off the edge of the earth. I keep telling them the world is round."

Wilma pointed out to sea. "Is that land over there?"

"I'M GOING TO BE FAMOUS!"

"I've done it! I've discovered a New World!" Columbus shouted joyfully.

By now the inventor of the time machine was most distressed. "This is terrible. I've got to bring those people back."

He shut his eyes and spun the dial again, holding his breath in anticipation.

Once more the Flintstones and Rubbles were transported through time.

THAT PERSON IS ACTUALLY FLYING!

THERE MUST BE A TRICK TO IT.

"Look at that sign," said Fred. "We're back at the Bedrock Fair."

"But I don't remember any of this," Wilma said. "I guess we missed some of the exhibits in the House of Tomorrow."

"Anybody hungry?" Fred asked, walking over to a nearby kiosk. "Four brontosaurus burgers, please."

The waiter chuckled. "That'll be two rocks, heh, heh."

Fred put two rocks on the counter.

"What's this?" the waiter snapped.

"It's good Bedrock money," Fred replied.

THAT MAN FROM THE PREHISTORIC EXHIBIT LOOKS SO AUTHENTIC.

"Look pal, give me some real money or I'll call the police," said the waiter.

Fred didn't know what to do.

The waiter shouted, "Police!"

The Flintstones and Rubbles dashed into the Time Tunnel to hide.

STOP RIGHT THERE!

THINK YOUR TIME MACHINE NEEDS A BIT MORE WORK!

Meanwhile, the inventor gave the time machine one last spin.

"If those people don't come back this time, I don't know what I'll do," he said.

Suddenly, Fred raced out of the time machine, followed by Betty, Wilma and Barney.

Later that day, the Flintstones and Rubbles drove home from the Bedrock Fair.

"So, what did you think of the future, Fred?" asked Barney.

"Let me put it this way," Fred replied. "The future is a nice place to visit, but I wouldn't want to live there!"

Swimming Pool Pranks

Barney and Fred had had an argument. They still weren't speaking, so Barney decided to collect some things Fred had borrowed from him.

"Oh and er, I need the ladder too, Wilma," said Barney.

"Fine," said Wilma. "Help yourself."

Unfortunately, Fred was still using the ladder!

ARE YOU OK, FRED?

FINE BARNEY. I ENJOY SITTING IN HOLES IN EX-GOOD FRIEND'S GARDENS!

AARGH!

"Is that so?" said Fred, suddenly interested. "What would you say to the kind offer of a free extra half to your pool? That way, you get a pool twice as big!"

"How do you mean, Fred?" asked Barney.

"Why you . . ." said Fred, giving chase into Barney's garden.

"Hey, what's going on?" he yelled as he fell into an enormous hole. "What are you doing Barney? What's the crater for?"

"I'm building a swimming pool, Fred," said Barney.

WALL

"I mean, old pal and esteemed neighbour, that if I have half the pool in my garden you'll have a bigger pool for the same money - right?"

THANKS, FRED.

JUST TO SHOW I'M RIGHT BEHIND YOU, HERE'S A PRESENT.

DO IT YOURSELF TOOL KIT

"Er, right, Fred," said Barney.
"Good thinking, Barney!"
So, poor Barney dug the whole pool - including Fred's half.

"Now, all it needs is filling, Barney boy. 4000 buckets should do it. I'll give you a hand with the first one just to show you what a big hearted guy I am!

Can't stop, Barney - time to get a few new swimming togs. See you later. Just think Barney - barbecues, swimming parties - it's going to be great!"

"Just think," said Barney wearily, as he trudged up and down.

When Fred drew up outside the cave later, Barney called out: "Hey Fred! This is the last bucket!"

SOMETHING TELLS ME THIS POOL IS GOING TO CAUSE PROBLEMS!

"Oh boy, oh boy, I'll race you in, Barney! Yabba dabba doo!"

YOU'RE ONE OF THE GOOD ONES, FRED.

ONLY 3999 BUCKETS TO GO, BARNEY!

Later Fred was relaxing in the pool on his airbed. "Oh honey," he called, "do you think you can bring my lunch out here? I'm just so comfortable!"

"Oh all right, Fred," sighed Wilma.

"Aaahhh! What's that?" she shrieked.

When Fred and Barney dived in, they missed the pool - but not each other!

"What do you think of my new spear fishing outfit, Wilma?" giggled Barney.

"Terrific, Barney. You'll scare the fish to death," said Wilma.

The pool was a big hit - especially with Barney's friends. Almost every day, Fred came home looking forward to a long cool swim, only to find the pool full.

"Who is it today, Barney?" asked Fred sarcastically.

"The YCMA, Fred - Young Cavemen's Association. They're having a great time!"

"That's it!" said Fred, stomping off towards his cave. "I'm not having my half of the pool used by everyone in the neighbourhood!"

Two hours later, Fred had put up a fence across the pool.

"Time to enjoy my half of the pool in peace," he said, and changed for a swim.

What he didn't know was that after the Young Cavemen's Association party broke up, Barney had drained his half of the water out of the pool, so Fred ended up in a nose dive!

Fred was relaxing indoors when he overheard Betty and Wilma talking about yet another party!

"I've had enough," muttered Fred. "Time to stop this joking around with one of my jokes!"

He picked up the phone and dialled. "Is that you Charlie?" he said.

"Hi, Fred," said Charlie. "How's things?"

Fred giggled as he explained what he wanted Charlie to do.

"That's fixed it for Barney and his party! Heh! Heh! Heh!" said Fred as he hung up the phone.

Lots of people arrived for the party, and then there was a knock at Fred's front door.

When he opened it, Barney and Betty stood there.

"What's the cake for?" growled Fred.

When they started singing, Fred didn't know what to say.

"Surprise, surprise!" said Barney. "This party's for you!"

38

The party was a great success, but they didn't notice the music was getting louder and louder.

It got so loud that an angry neighbour called the police.

When the two police officers arrived a few moments later, Fred didn't worry.

"Charlie! Glad you could make it - and a friend too! No need for the disturbing the peace routine - just join in!"

"Me? Why? I mean, that's real kind of you - play the drums Barney, and I'll take the strings - this is going to be some party!"

HELLO, POLICE? COME TO 342 GRAVEL PIT TERRACE AT ONCE - THEY'RE DISTURBING THE PEACE!

LOOKS LIKE BARNEY AND FRED HAVE FINALLY STOPPED QUARRELLING!

"My name's not Charlie, and if you don't stop this party now, I'm going to run you in!"

"Oh, I get it - I'll go along with the gag, Charlie," whispered Fred. "Right," he shouted, "just watch me run *you* in!"

Fred heard a small voice beside him.
"Hi, Fred."
"Oh, hi Charlie - Charlie!"

"I couldn't get the police suit - thought I'd come to the party anyway."

"This party's over," said the other police officer. "Get in the car, Mr Flintstone!"

"What a disaster!" moaned Fred as he sat in the police cell later. "I didn't even get a piece of my cake!"

"Psst, Fred," said Barney. "We'll get you out of here in a jiffy. In the meantime, here's something for you."

"You're one of the good ones, Barney," sighed Fred.

"Just think of it this way, Fred," said Barney. "You're going to miss loads of turns at cleaning out the pool!"

Ring-a-Ding

"Nothing like that, Fred. See, I've just bought Betty a ring for our anniversary present, but it's a secret until we celebrate at the weekend. Can you look after it for me?"

"OK, Barney," said Fred, "It'll be safe with me!"

Fred went back indoors to find a safe hiding place for the ring.

"I don't want Wilma to find it and blab to Betty. The flour tin's a good place. We don't do much baking anymore."

OH BOY, WHAT A ROCK. IT MUST HAVE COST A FORTUNE!

Barney stuck his head through Fred's window one day looking very suspicious.

"Psst, Fred, come out here. I want to ask you a favour," he whispered.

"If it's money you want, Barney, I'm broke."

"Fred!" said Wilma taking him by surprise. "What are you doing up there?"

"Oh, er, hi Wilma. I er, saw a mouse, but it er, ran away," said Fred.

"Are you sure, Fred?" said Wilma.

Later, Fred heard Wilma moving around in the kitchen.

"Oh great, sounds like Wilma is making a cake - a cake!" he realised, jumping up. "Hey, Wilma! Stop that!"

To Wilma's horror, Fred grabbed the flour tin and ran with it.

He closed the door and tipped out the flour, but Betty's ring wasn't there.

"Fred! Fred! Will you come out of the bedroom this minute!" yelled Wilma. "Go and have a shower - perhaps that will cool you down!"

When the cake went into the oven, Wilma popped round to Betty's. Fred decided to retrieve the ring from the cake, but when he opened the oven door, the cake fell flat.

Then Wilma walked in. She was furious. She threw out the cake and put it outside in the rubbish.

42

"That was lucky," she said when she came back, "the dustcart was collecting."

"Yipes!" said Fred, pushing Wilma out of the way.

"Perhaps Fred's been working too hard," thought Wilma picking herself up. "He's acting very strangely!"

Fred ran to catch up with the dustcart. He rummaged through the rubbish until he found the ring.

"Got it! Thanks, buddy," said Fred to the driver, getting off the cart.

"What a fruitcake. Whoever heard of hijacking a dustcart?" muttered the driver.

Back home, Fred was looking for another place to hide the ring.

"Wilma will never find it in this old bowling ball - I'll go and tell Barney."

Later, Wilma was looking for something when she saw the old bowling ball.

"Why does Fred keep that thing? It's no use." As she picked it up, the ring fell out.

OK, BUSTER, THIS IS A STICK UP. PUT YOUR HANDS UP AND DON'T TURN ROUND.

BLESS HIS FAT LITTLE HEART. HE MUST HAVE SAVED UP FOR AGES!

"Oh! A ring - for me! So *that's* why he's been so secretive. I must show Betty."

"Oh Wilma, you are lucky," sighed Betty when saw the ring. "When did Fred give it to you?"

"He hasn't yet - I found where he'd hidden it. I must put it back now - I don't want to spoil his surprise," giggled Wilma.

But when Fred came back, Wilma couldn't help telling him she'd found the ring.

"Oh Fred- I'm so happy, I'm all choked up," she said.

"Oh boy," muttered Fred, "when Barney finds out he's going to choke *me* up!"

"There's nothing for it, Fred," said Barney when Fred had told him the story. "We'll have to go to the jewellers and buy another ring that I can give to Betty."

But when Fred found out how much the ring cost, his heart sank. "Where am I going to get £500?" he moaned.

"What about that, Fred?" said Barney, pointing to a poster.

"Go three minutes with The Champ? Brilliant idea, Barney - but not me - you!"

"Why me?" wailed Barney.

"Because you're faster on your feet!"

Betty and Wilma went shopping and met a friend. When they found out that the ring hadn't been bought for Wilma, they went to the jewellers to find out exactly what was going on.

"All I know is the little guy is going to do three minutes with The Champ to get £500!" said the jeweller.

"Barney's got to win that match," said Betty to the fight organiser. "Here's £500 I've saved up. That way, when Barney wins the money, you'll still have £500."

"OK, OK, lady," said the organiser.

But when they'd gone, he turned to The Champ. "Sock it to him as usual, kid. That way we've got an extra £500! Heh! Heh!"

Barney was very nervous before the fight.

"I'm right behind you, Barney!" yelled Fred.

"That's no use!" said Barney, clinging on as Fred dragged him into the ring.

Ding Ding! The first round had started.

THWACK!! The Champ landed an enormous punch on Barney's jaw and he went out cold. Fred tried desperately to bring Barney round.

Betty and Wilma had decided to come and see the fight too.

"I'll give that Champ what for!" said Wilma. The Champ was so surprised, he didn't prepare himself for the blow and Wilma's right hook knocked him out - right out of the ring!

"You crook!" yelled Betty, as the organiser tried to sneak away. "You said that Barney would win! Give them the £500!"

Betty and Wilma made sure the fight organiser went to see Fred and Barney.

"I er, owe you this, lads. When we er, counted up the time, you lasted three minutes just fine. The money's yours!"

So Fred took the money and bought Barney another ring to give to Betty.

And Wilma used her money to take them all to the beach for the weekend.

"You guys are terrific," said Wilma, lazing on the sand.

"That goes for you girls too - real knockout!" laughed Fred.

The Trail of the Snorkasaurus

"Six dodo eggs, pterodactyl soup, some marsh greens..."

Fred was hard at work at the Bedrock Quarry Co. He heard the telephone ring and then a voice called: "Hey Fred! It's Wilma for you!"

"Hi, honey. What's up? You want me to do some shopping? OK, Wilma, I'll stop off at the supermarket on the way home."

"Hi buddy!" called Barney when Fred arrived at the supermarket. "What are you doing here?"

"What do you think I'm doing, watching my hair grow? Shopping, working, charging around - that's all I seem to do these days. Hey, I've just had a great idea! Come home with me and we can tell Betty and Wilma!"

"So, what's the brainwave, Fred?" asked Wilma.

"We're all busy, right? So what we all need is a break, right?"

DINOSAUR STEAKS
BRONTO BURGERS

"Oh great! I love the beach!" said Betty.

"No, no - a real change, up in the mountains - fresh air, sleeping in tents."

"In tents?" chorused Wilma and Betty. They definitely weren't keen on the idea.

"I don't see what's wrong with the beach, Fred. We go every year," continued Wilma.

"Exactly," said Fred triumphantly. "Time for a change!"

Fred was still snoring next morning when Wilma pushed him into the car.

"Wha . . . whassa matter?" he murmured sleepily.

"It's the early start, Fred - just like you said we must have!" muttered Wilma, closing the door before Fred could fall out of the car.

Barney had packed all his sports gear into the trailer. They would have needed the entire garage to take everything he wanted, and first time round, the trailer was jammed so tightly inside, it stopped them pulling away!

They headed for the hills, but no-one noticed that the trailer had broken loose from its coupling.

"Er, Fred, where's the trailer gone?" asked Barney.

"Don't bother me, Barney. I'm trying to get past this enormous trailer in front of us - boy, is he slow!"

"Fred, that's *our* trailer," said Wilma.

"Well, why didn't someone tell me?" shouted Fred. "Am I the only one who can do anything round here?"

When they arrived, Fred and Barney set about making camp.

"Hey, Fred, I'll chop us some wood just like they do in the movies!" giggled Barney.

"Fine, Barney, fine. I'll go and see what tracks I can find - we're going looking for that Snorkasaurus tomorrow, old pal!"

Wilma and Betty put up the tents.

"Barney," called Betty, "that tree is going to . . ."

Too late. Barney had let the tree fall right on top of the trailer!

Next, Barney tried his hand at fishing. "Just wait, Fred. I'll catch us a fish just as soon as you can say . . ."

"Mmm, what's that Barney?" muttered Fred, who was trying to start a fire. But things didn't go quite according to plan.

"Barney, help! Barney - come here, where are you?" shrieked Fred as he scorched himself.

"Over here, Fred - looks like, er the fish caught me, eh Fred?"

At the end of an exhausting day, everyone was ready to go to bed early.

"I found the trail of the Snorkasaurus in those woods. So it's another early start tomorrow, Barney boy, and we can get down to some serious tracking."

"Why do we have to have an early start, Fred?" asked Barney.

"Because, er that's what you do when you track. Otherwise, er, you er, you er, miss the Snorkasaurus."

"Oh, I see, Fred. Goodnight Fred."

The next day, as Fred and Barney set off towards the forest for their tracking, the Snorkasaurus was waking up: "Ah, it is morning. Another day - and with the day, will come the chase. What sport!"

"Hey, Fred, what does this er, Snooker, Snorka thing look like?" puffed Barney.

"I'll draw you a picture," said Fred, picking up a stick. "Like this, look - he's got a big nose, a fat body and flat feet."

"No, no," said a voice behind them.

"Not at all," said the creature they saw when they looked up. "The Snorkasaurus is a handsome animal, with a regal head, strong body and large but neat feet. And famous for its melodious call."

Sniggering, the Snorkasaurus ran off into the distance.

"What was that, Fred?" asked Barney.

"Something tells me that was what we were looking for - after him!" yelled Fred, giving chase.

The Snorkasaurus ended up in their camp.

"Aha!" he said, when he spotted a tent. "A perfect shelter for a poor hunted creature like myself!"

The Snorkasaurus dived in only to be faced with Wilma and Betty. They screamed in fright.

"Oh dear, ladies, I did not mean to startle you. Take pity on me, poor creature that I am, at the mercy of two sturdy hunters pursuing me!"

Fred and Barney chased into the tent, following the Snorkasaurus tracks.

"So there you are!" they cried.

"Just a minute, Fred. Don't you dare lay a finger on this charming creature," said Wilma with a determined look.

"And that goes for you too, Barney!" shouted Betty.

COME ON, FRED. HE'S AWFULLY CUTE!

"Fred, we need a pet. He's perfect," said Wilma. "I'll call him Snorky."

"This monster?" asked Fred.

"Please give me a chance," pleaded the Snorkasaurus. "I can cook, sew, clean - I'll even carry your bowling ball!"

"How come I get the feeling I've got no say in this?" sighed Fred.

Back at home a few days later, the telephone rang.

"Hello. Flintstones' residence. Of course. Madam, it's for you."

"Thanks, Snorky. Hello. Oh, hi Betty. How are you?"

"Oh, fine," replied Betty. "I was just phoning to find out how Fred was getting on with his new pet."

"Just fine - as long as Snorky lets him win at bowling!"

Fred and the Magic Cabinet

I KNOW EVERYONE ENJOYS MY SINGING, BUT THIS YEAR I WANT TO DO SOMETHING DIFFERENT

YOUR SINGING CERTAINLY IS SOMETHING DIFFERENT, FRED.

Fred and Barney were trying to decide what act they should each do for the Bedrock Annual Show.

"I want to surprise people this year," said Fred. "What are you going to do, Barney?"

"Don't know, Fred. I'll think of something."

"So will I, Barney, something better!"

"Could be, Fred!"

Fred decided he'd talk about it with Wilma when he got home.

"Why not sing as usual?" asked Wilma when Fred explained.

"Yeah, maybe you're right. People will be disappointed if I don't sing. After all . . ."

". . . you did sing in a rock band - twenty years ago!" interrupted Wilma. "You're always reminding us!"

Fred decided to jog Wilma's memory one more time.

"Practise your singing outside, Fred!" yelled Wilma above the noise. "The plates can't stand it and neither can I!"

Fred went to sulk in the garden. As he relaxed in the sun, he saw Barney over the garden wall. Then Barney disappeared . . . and re-appeared . . . and disappeared . . .

"What are you doing, Barney?" asked Fred curiously.

"Trampolining, Fred. Want to try?"

YOU WIN, BARNEY. BUT I'LL IMPROVE WITH PRACTICE, THEN I'LL SHOW WILMA MY TRAMPOLINING ACT!

WHAT DID I TELL YOU, FRED?

"Great idea! I'm coming over!" said Fred.

"No, Fred, don't jump from the garden wall. You'll bounce . . ."

BOINGG! Fred flew into the air and landed in a tree nearby.

". . . too high!" finished Barney.

Fred had forgotten Wilma was visiting the dressmaker that afternoon.

"That's no problem. I'll show her there. Boy, will she get a surprise when she sees me through the window!"

Quickly, Fred set up the trampoline and started bouncing.

AARGH!

"Yes, madam, this is our latest model . . . aargh! There's someone peeping in!" shrieked the dressmaker.

"Outside?" said Wilma "But that's impossible! We're on the second fl . . . Fred!"

She stuck her head out of the window as she suddenly realised who was causing the trouble!

IF THIS IS ANOTHER IDEA FOR THE SHOW, YOU CAN FORGET IT!

"Oh no? Watch this. The hand is quicker than the eye!"

CRASH!

"More broken plates! Magic's no good either Fred!"

"What's the noise?" asked Barney and Betty.

"Oh nothing," said Fred. "Just - er, practising my magic."

Fred still didn't have an act. But by the time Wilma came home, he'd had another brilliant idea.

"What's all this junk?" asked Wilma.

"Junk? You call this junk?" replied Fred. "I've borrowed this *equipment* from Rockstone the Magician."

"But Fred, you don't know anything about magic."

"What's that?" asked Barney, peering over Fred's shoulder.

"That," said Fred impressively, "is my disappearing cabinet. Step forward and I shall astound you."

Betty persuaded Wilma to get inside with her, and Fred said the magic words.

Inside the cabinet, Wilma and Betty discovered a secret door. They stepped out through the back of the cabinet and went into the bedroom.

"Er, Fred, they've really gone!" said Barney when Fred opened the cabinet doors. "Bring them back!"

Fred grinned.

"How about a night out instead, Barney old pal? My old friend Hot Lips Hannigan is playing at Rockland. Let's go!"

"Did you hear that?" hissed Wilma as Barney and Fred got in the car. "I've never heard of anything so sneaky!"

"Don't worry, Wilma - we can go too! Put on those clothes we wore for the fancy dress party and they won't recognise us!"

At Rockland, Hot Lips was sending the crowd wild.

"Hi there, fans. Let's lift the roof off Rockland tonight!"

"Hey Hot Lips! Over here!" yelled Fred. "Remember me? It's Fred, Fred Flintstone!"

Hot Lips turned around in surprise.

"Fred! Long time, no see! What about getting up here with me and giving us a song - for old times' sake?"

"Oh, I don't know . . ."

"Oh come on Fred - do it for me!"

"What's going on?" muttered the crowd as Barney and Fred took the stage. "They look too old for this."

Fred and Barney started their number. Fred's voice didn't always hit the right notes, and Barney's drumming wasn't perfect, but soon everyone was enjoying themselves.

When Wilma and Betty arrived the crowd was screaming.

"Looks as though they're getting the real star treatment!" giggled Betty as they watched Fred and Barney being chased off stage by enthusiastic fans. "We'd better show them a way out."

"Psst, over here boys," whispered Wilma and Betty.

"Oh er, thanks, girls," said Fred and Barney. They didn't realise it was Wilma and Betty.

"You guys were terrific," said Wilma.

"You sure were - how about going out for a meal and some dancing?" said Betty.

Barney gulped as Betty gave him a kiss. "Er, look girls, thanks for the invitation," said Fred, "but we've got another engagement - now!"

Fred and Barney leaped into Fred's car and drove home at top speed.

"We've got to get Betty and Wilma back from that cabinet, fast!" said Fred.

With a flourish, Fred said the magic words and opened the doors of the cabinet.

"Well, hello boys." Betty and Wilma stood there, still in disguise.

"Let's get out of here!"

Fred and Barney ran into the next room and slammed the door behind them.

Slowly, they peeped round the door.

"They're gone. If Wilma and Betty ever caught us with those . . ."

"With who, Fred?" asked Wilma stepping forward.

She and Betty had changed back into their normal clothes.

"Oh, Wilma, am I glad to see you!" said Fred. But the relief was too much for Fred. He keeled over in a faint!

"Are you all right, Fred?" asked Wilma innocently when Fred came round.

"Sure - it's all that magic - takes it out of me," whispered Fred.

"That was some disappearing act, Fred," said Betty, secretly winking at Wilma. "Are you going to do that for the show?"

"Oh, no. I'll stick to trampolining or singing - or even pterodactyl juggling - anything's safer than that cabinet! Take it back to Rockstone the Great, Barney - right now!"

Stories first published 1991, 1992 by Buzz Books,
an imprint of Reed Consumer Books Limited
Michelin House, 81 Fulham Road, London SW3 6RB
and Auckland, Melbourne, Singapore and Toronto

This edition first published in Great Britain 1993 by Dean,
in association with Heinemann Young Books

ISBN 0 603 55101 7

A CIP record for this book is available at the British Library

Produced by Mandarin
Printed in China